CHAPTER ONE
A fright in the night

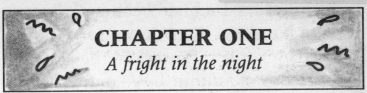

I jolted awake in
my bed.

The noise came from out in the garden.

Only yesterday Dad had been growling about a burglary, three doors down our street. Thieves had ransacked the place, taking loads of antiques. We didn't have any antiques, but Dad had a cabinet stuffed full of silver trophies. He had once been a roller-skate champion.

The Baked Bean Cure

Philip Wooderson and Dee Shulman

Collins

JUMBO JETS

Bernie Works a Miracle · Leon Rosselson and Kate Sheppard
Fergus the Forgetful · Margaret Ryan and Wendy Smith
Forecast of Fear · Keith Brumpton
Pickles Sniffs it Out · Michaela Morgan and Dee Shulman
The Man in Shades · Pat Thomson and Caroline Crossland
Sir Quinton Quest Hunts the Yeti · Kaye Umansky and Judy Brown
Sir Quinton Quest Hunts the Jewel · Kaye Umansky and Judy Brown
Trouble on the Day · Norma Clarke and Peter Kavanagh

First published in Great Britain by
A & C Black (Publishers) Ltd in 1995
First published by Collins in 1996

9 8 7 6 5 4 3 2 1

Collins is an imprint of HarperCollins*Publishers* Ltd,
77-85 Fulham Palace Road, Hammersmith, London W6 8JB.

Text copyright © Philip Wooderson 1995
Illustrations copyright © Dee Shulman 1995

000 675101 6

Printed and bound in Great Britain by
HarperCollins Manufacturing, Glasgow

I hastily climbed out of bed.

There was a bright full moon, casting long black shadows over the lawn. It looked peaceful. But just to make perfectly sure, I eased the window open and, leaning over the sill, I took a look down and I saw . . .

an overturned flowerpot

a rucksack

and someone peering in through our kitchen window.

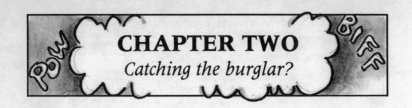

CHAPTER TWO
Catching the burglar?

I blundered across the landing into my parents' room.

That brought Dad round. He jerked upright.

Before I'd got started on 'Where?' he threw himself out of bed. I chased him down the stairs and saw him disappear into the front room. When he bobbed out again he was clutching a heavy brass poker. No flies on Dad. He was armed now. And at an incredible pace he strode across the kitchen, unlocked the door and stepped out.

Then silence.

Just as I reached the conclusion that Dad and the horrible burglar had knocked each other for six, I heard Dad's voice again.

'I've got him – quick, turn on the light.'

I fumbled and found the switch. The strip light flickered and blinked. What I saw was a gangly person wearing tattered blue jeans and a dirty jacket.

OH NO.

IT WAS UNCLE MERVYN.

CHAPTER THREE
My Uncle Merv

My uncle was worse than a burglar. He couldn't be clamped in handcuffs and marched off by the police. More likely he'd stay here for weeks,

raiding
the fridge
every
night

and leaving brown scum in the bath.

Dad would grind his teeth but – Uncle Merv was Mum's elder brother.

I think he did odd jobs, to save up to go on his travels. But now he was back, from India. He'd missed the last bus from the station and here he was in our kitchen at quarter-to-one in the morning.

I dare say you're starving, Merv.

Well, if it's no trouble...

Of course not! We're glad to see you.

Dad guided him into a chair and hurried to put the kettle on.

You've chosen a very good moment.

I got the message.

You see, Dad had booked a break for Mum and himself in the country, to give Mum a much-needed rest. I hadn't really minded because the plan had been for Granny to come to stay. But, yesterday, Granny had got the flu so Mum and Dad's trip was postponed, unless . . .

'Oh pooh!' Dad said with a grin. 'You just have to keep all the doors shut.'

'But what about Ben?' said Mum, meaning my much-younger brother. 'To start with, he's a fusspot. The things he won't eat, a whole list, and . . .'

'Darling, he'll live on baked beans.'

'He shouldn't, though. I've been trying –'

'A challenge', crowed Uncle Merv. 'I'll wean him off trashy canned beans. I'll cook up some decent wholefoods. That is, if you'd . . . ?'

It makes me sick to admit this, but after breakfast on Thursday, my mother and father set off, leaving their own dear children at the mercy of Uncle Merv.

It wasn't too bad to start with –

> Gee up Neddy.

> Nice sounds Tony.

But early that afternoon Uncle said he would pop into town.

'What about burglars?' I asked him.
'I mean, if they're watching the house?'

> I've got to get food for the weekend - I'll only be gone fifteen minutes.

He wasn't. He stayed out for hours.
So I had to look after Ben.

When Uncle came back at last, he had
some silly excuse about making friends
with two people he'd met in the health
food shop. He was clutching a carrier bag
that was crammed full of packets and
bottles. He set them all out on the table.

It's like something that brings about changes inside of yourself. It's a potion. Two spoonfuls every mealtime from now on. It'll totally clear out the system.

I gazed at the three black bottles, each priced at £4.99.

But what about food?

I forgot that.

The only things in the kitchen that Uncle considered 'wholefoods' were three gigantic potatoes he found in a bag in the cupboard. Everything else, he decided, would have to come fresh from the garden.

Dad wasn't a vegetable gardener. We only had grass and shrubs.

But Uncle said things that grew wild made incredible salads.

16

Then I got stung on the wrist and Uncle got really excited.

Nettles! – they make a great soup. WOW!

They didn't. At least, he didn't. He made a disgusting, foul soup that not even he could eat.

This left us with baked potatoes, or what I'd call 'half-baked potatoes' that hadn't been properly washed, and Uncle's 'Incredible Salad', made from dandelion leaves.

The whole feast was chewy and bitter,
with crunchy lumps of earth, but worse –

It didn't help me in the least, to hear him burbling on about how he'd heard of an island in the Indian Ocean where the people loved slugs, stir-fried with bean shoots and mushrooms.

I tottered out into the garden holding my hands to my mouth, trying to think about nice things . . .

. . . then I looked down the garden path.

I saw a spidery figure
leaning over the gate.
He was wearing a
black leather jacket.
I swear he'd been
watching the house.

What do
you want?

He dodged out of sight
and scurried off
down the alley.

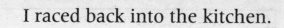

I raced back into the kitchen.

Uncle, I've just seen a burglar casing the joint, quick - **hurry!**

Uncle grinned like a sheep. 'More likely a neighbour, Tony, out walking his dog. Mellow down.'

Before I could ask him what that meant, Ben tipped his wholefood supper over the edge of his high-chair, on to Uncle's lap.

Don't want it, can't like it. I'm **HUNGRY!**

So what do you fancy?

BEANS!

CHAPTER SIX
More natural goodness

It took Uncle Merv several minutes to wipe the wholefoods off his jeans.

Then Ben got his beans. So did I.

He reached for the Natural Elixir.

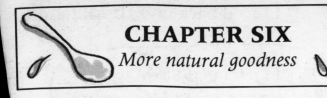
It took Uncle Merv several minutes to wipe the wholefoods off his jeans.

Then Ben got his beans. So did I.

But don't you want any, Uncle?

I only eat **healthy** food.

He reached for the Natural Elixir.

It didn't help me in the least, to hear him burbling on about how he'd heard of an island in the Indian Ocean where the people loved slugs, stir-fried with bean shoots and mushrooms.

I tottered out into the garden holding my hands to my mouth, trying to think about nice things . . .

. . . then I looked down the garden path.

I saw a spidery figure leaning over the gate. He was wearing a black leather jacket. I swear he'd been watching the house.

What do you want?

ht

I raced back into the kitchen

Uncle, I've just seen a burglar casing the joint, quick - hurry!

Uncle grinned like a sheep. 'More lik neighbour, Tony, out walking his do Mellow down.'

Before I could ask him what that m Ben tipped his wholefood supper o edge of his high-chair, on to Uncle

Don't want it, can't like it. I'm HUNGRY!

so what do you fancy?

BEANS!

It stuck to my tongue and rolled down my throat like treacle, leaving an after-taste that suddenly twisted round and went all bitter and sour.

I got up and spat in the sink.

He sloped off into the lounge.

I tipped those 'wholefoods' in the bin, took Ben up to bed, then came down to wash the dishes. It all took a fair bit of time. Time enough to think about that man by the gate. He certainly wasn't a neighbour.

Did he know Mum and Dad were away? What better time to break in? He might even try it tonight. I had to make Uncle see sense.

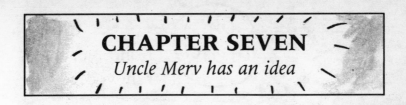

As soon as I entered the lounge I was hit by a bilious stink.

Oh, great!

I said, very relieved.

You think we should call the police?

I mean The Answer for Ben... To stop him from eating baked beans.

Oh no, I could hardly believe this. 'Why not just stop giving him beans?'

'He'd want them even more then. I've had a much better idea. We give him beans every meal – until he gets bored with beans. But we'd better eat them as well. That way he won't think that he's special.'

I wondered. At least if we ate beans we wouldn't have to live on 'wholefoods'.

He gave me a long, tired look.

CHAPTER EIGHT
The bean regime

I hardly slept that night. I lay awake straining my ears for any odd creak or bump. It's amazing how noisy our house is. But I drifted off in the end and woke up much later than usual.

Downstairs, I found Uncle Merv.

He's already had 3 helpings. Come on, Tony, tuck into this.

But aren't you having some too?

It's funny, I never eat breakfast.

Uncle spent the rest of the morning
watching a cowboy film. I spent it
scrubbing the bean pan and playing with
Ben. Very boring.

For lunch there were  . . . again.

At tea-time we
had more . . .

Ben had LOTS more . . .

He was having a wonderful time.

Uncle ate only one small helping. His treat was the Natural Elixir. I watched him swallow it down.

What's more, he didn't go green. He hummed peculiar tunes. He even played 'Monsters' with Ben . . .

. . . until it was way past his bedtime.

CHAPTER NINE
A stricter regime

On Friday night I slept like a log. Even the heaviest burglar could have tripped over my bed and I'd have known nothing about it.

In the morning,
Ben woke me up,
so I took him downstairs
for his breakfast.

ROAR!! WAAH!

We couldn't wake Uncle up.

zzzz

BOING!

He was snoring away like a hippo.

I made sure Dad's trophies were safe,
then made the breakfast myself.

If Mum had
been here to
see me, she
would have
gone through
the roof.

Ben guzzled
helpings of beans. He did.
I couldn't believe it.

His mouth went traffic-light orange.
When Uncle slouched into the
kitchen, I thought it
was time to
warn him –

Your cure's not going to work.

34

He yawned.

I've thought about that I've been up all night. Here's **The Answer.**

Yes?

Doses of beans between meals — snacks, to speed up the cure.

I didn't like this at all.

What, beans at elevenses time?

Slurp!

We gave it a try. Ben managed two extra helpings instead of a chocolate biscuit. But well before half-past twelve he thought it was time for his . . . 'BEANS!' This might not matter to Uncle. He seemed to live on thin air and Runneymeade's Natural Elixir. But I'd lived on nothing but beans for five meals on the trot, and I was properly cured. I longed to eat anything else, even a half-baked potato, but –

There was only one can left.

'I'll go to the shops', said Merv. 'You got any money, Tony?'

I'll pay if I can go. And you stay and look after Ben.

'I don't think your dad would like that.'

He wouldn't, no. Not if I told him what you spent on your Natural Elixir!

This seemed to do the trick.

Okay babe, I'll soothe you with sounds.

CHAPTER TEN
Early warning

I needed some advice, so after stocking up with beans at the corner shop, I went off to find my mate Dwayne.

He's known as Brayne-Dwayne at school, because he's so intellectual. He said Uncle's cure wouldn't work.

It'll make Ben a baked bean **ADDICT**. You need to muck up the flavour. Sabotage each can.

Before he could tell me what that meant,
a couple of men pushed past:

I stared at Dwayne, thinking fast.

Our house was in Haverstock Road.

Mum and Dad would be back Sunday evening.

The man who had said 'it' was 'on' had been wearing a black leather jacket.

I left Dwayne and hurried back home. Uncle wasn't the least bit pleased when I claimed I'd seen burglars again.

Like, 20 minutes ago, the guy I met in the health shop phoned up and asked himself over.

I said, "We'll have a tea party".

BEANS!

Okay - a BEANS party!

Of course we had beans that night too; beans for the seventh meal running. I managed a couple of forkfuls and Ben packed away all the rest. Uncle ate nothing at all.

Food only clouds the brain.

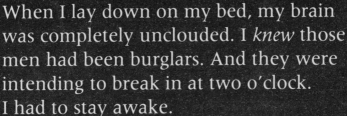

CHAPTER ELEVEN
Burglar alarm

When I lay down on my bed, my brain was completely unclouded. I *knew* those men had been burglars. And they were intending to break in at two o'clock.
I had to stay awake.
Easier said than done. When I next opened my eyes, the clock said `1 55`

I tensed. I was hearing strange noises. Not minor creaks or rustlings or late night cars swishing past, but clatter and clanking downstairs.

I crept down those stairs like a ghost.

A hissing sound came from the kitchen. My heart was thumping hard, but I carefully twisted the knob and nudged the door slightly open.

I saw Uncle straight away.

I saw what was piled on his plate. It made me so giddy with hunger that I would have thrown myself forwards and begged him to share his huge fry-up, if I hadn't been so *cross*.

No wonder he'd skipped through the daytime on less than a spoonful of beans. He was saving himself for later. Uncle Merv was a rotten old fraud.

But while I was taking this in, I saw something even more startling.

Uncle Merv took a gi-normous great slurp
of Elixir.

He took another.

And then a third.

And a fourth.

He should have gone
up in blue smoke.
That stuff was foul,
it was poison, and
yet he could gulp it,
for *fun*?

I'd met my match.

I backed out.

46

CHAPTER TWELVE
Unnatural elixir

I couldn't go back to sleep, so when I got
up on Sunday morning I was at least
fairly sure that no burglars had broken in.
I was less sure about Uncle. I hoped that
his midnight feast had only been a
strange dream, but when I went down for
breakfast I found the evidence.

I felt so swizzled and diddled, I swore that
from then on I would eat whatever I
wanted.

And you,
Ben —
Cocoa Pops?

BEANS!

I loved my brother. I didn't want him growing up to be a baked bean freak.

I had to do something to cure him of Uncle's baked bean cure before Mum and Dad got back.

Perhaps Dwayne's idea would work, but how was I going to make the beans taste really horrid?

I rummaged all over the kitchen, until I found just what I needed, right in front of my eyes.

Bitter as poison ...

but harmless

It must be, the way Uncle quaffed it.

This bottle was nearly empty.

I took a sniff. It smelt malty, a bit like Christmas pudding but nothing like Natural Elixir. In fact it reminded me of something my Dad rather liked. What was going on here?

Uncle was snooZing as I tiptoed across the lounge and z opened the base of the cabinet where Z Dad kept his bottles and glasses.

The brand-new bottle of whisky that Mum had bought for Dad's birthday only a week ago was now very nearly empty.

Beside it, the other two bottles of Runneymeade's Natural Elixir were full. They hadn't been opened.

Uncle was trying to fool me that he was taking his 'medicine' while swigging Dad's drinks on the sly!

This was war! Can you guess what I did?

I poured the last of Dad's whisky into the rubber plant pot and replaced it with Natural Elixir from one of those two spare bottles.

When Uncle feels thirsty again, he'll have a gut-fizzling surprise!

CHAPTER THIRTEEN
Shock to the system

I needed to catch up on some sleep so, leaving Ben in his playpen not too far from Uncle, I hopped it up to my room. When I lay down and shut my eyes, all I could see were beans floating in bright orange sauce. I counted more than a hundred before I slipped into a doze.

The next thing I knew it was tea-time, and I could hear voices downstairs. I guessed Uncle's friends must have come. Curious, I got out of bed and went down to have a look, but the door to the lounge was shut.

I felt too shy to burst in, so I crept out through the kitchen, deciding to spy on them first.

They were sitting on the settee, watching as Uncle Merv poured three tumblers of 'whisky'.

Gulp – no, double gulp. I recognised those men.

But now I could see they weren't burglars. They were Uncle's FRIENDS.

What I had overheard, outside Brayne-Dwayne's house, had only been them planning to come and have some tea!

But my Uncle was going to give them something stronger than tea. Stronger than he realised. What was I going to do?

I stumbled back into the kitchen.

Yaqowwww!

Oh no, that was Uncle. He must have swallowed a dose. His friends wouldn't risk it, not now. But the rumpus was getting much louder . . . Uncle was thrashing and screaming. Supposing the stuff did him in?

I threw myself into the lounge, ready to phone for an ambulance but . . .

I sprang back. What should I do? Beat it and phone the police? I couldn't leave Ben with the . . . burglars.

I dithered a moment too long.

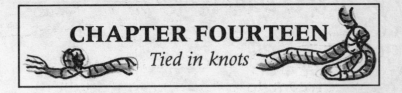

Dragged back into the lounge I saw Ben still in his playpen, hugging his teddybear. I glared at Uncle. He winced.

I'm sorry. I misread the vibes.

Put a sock in it, hippy. There's work to be done. Hold the kid, Trev.

I watched him loading Dad's trophies into Uncle's old rucksack.

While Trev held onto my elbows the Jacket ransacked the lounge, turning out drawers and cupboards, spilling stuff onto the carpet.

I thought of the mess they would make.
Then, Jacket remembered the 'whisky'.
He handed a tumbler to Trev.

They swallowed it down in one.

A couple of seconds went by.

Grabbing hold of his paunch Trev did a
little dance while Jacket doubled up,
dropping down on his knees to gurgle

Trev started to go round in circles, like a
clockwork mouse. He didn't look where
he was going, and tripped over
Uncle Merv.

This seemed like the
moment to leg it.

Out in the street I kept
running, intending to
head for a call-box. Before
I could reach it, however,

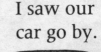

I saw our
car go by.

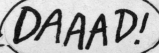

As Dad climbed out, looking rested,
I threw myself into his arms.

I must have hit the right note. Dad went
off like a firework – whizz – through the
open front door.

CHAPTER FIFTEEN
The baked bean cure

After he'd untied Uncle Merv, Dad used the ropes on the burglars. They didn't try to stop him. Mum dialled 999.

Within about fifteen minutes those burglars were led off in handcuffs, leaving us in the hands of two very nosy detectives.

'Don't fuss yourselves', said a detective. 'What matters is catching those villains. And I've got a funny feeling that your son knows more than he's letting on.'

Before Dad could think about that, Mum burst into the lounge. Her white T-shirt was spattered with beans.

I swopped worried glances with Uncle.

She broke off to gulp a quick breath –

She threw her arms around Merv and gave him a smacking great kiss.

I thought of those socks,

his Big Fry-Up,

and the 'natural elixir' I'd nearly poured into Ben's beans.

Things might have turned out worse.

My head's a little bit cloudy...

Oh Tony!

Mum let go of Uncle and gave me a wonderful hug.

I don't suppose you'd have noticed if he'd given you beans *every* meal.!